Shipwrecked on Mystery Island

Shipwrecked on Mystery Island

BY ROY WANDELMAIER

Illustrated by J. Brian Pinkney

Library of Congress Cataloging in Publication Data

Wandelmaier, Roy.
    Shipwrecked on Mystery Island.

    Summary: You are shipwrecked on a beautiful Pacific
island in 1869 and must choose a course of events that
will get you off, keep you there, or, indeed, ensure
that you survive at all.
    1. Plot-your-own stories. 2. Children's stories,
American. [1. Shipwrecked—Fiction. 2. Fantasy.
3. Plot-your-own stories] I. Pinkney, J. Brian, ill.
II. Title.
PZ7.W179Sh   1985   [Fic]   85-2531
ISBN 0-8167-0533-X (lib. bdg.)
ISBN 0-8167-0534-8 (pbk.)

We Hope You Enjoy
This Adventure Story

Just remember to read it differently than you would most other books. Start on page 1 and keep reading till you come to a choice. After that the story is up to you. Your decisions will take you from page to page.

Think carefully before you decide. Some choices will lead you to exciting, heroic, and happy endings. But watch out! Other choices can quickly lead to disaster.

Now you are ready to begin. The best of luck in your adventure!

Shipwrecked on Mystery Island

The year is 1869. You are sailing on the cargo ship, *Sacramento*, bound for Melbourne, Australia, to visit your uncle Jack.

You have been at sea two and a half weeks, and are now in the very center of the Pacific Ocean. When you wake up in your small berth this morning, your body feels stiff. You go to stretch your legs up on deck. The early morning sky is red, and the sea breeze is turning into a strong wind. A storm is building. By afternoon, your ship is in the middle of a terrible storm.

The sailors quickly haul down the sails, and you help try to latch things down. But it is no use. The hurricane winds snap off the mainsail, and huge waves wash over the deck. Three sailors are swept overboard.

The next tremendous wave overturns the *Sacramento*. You do all you can to hang on to a barrel, but you are pitched into the churning sea. The barrel is now your only hope for survival. Night comes quickly, and soon you do not hear the voices of any of the crew. Holding on to the barrel, you drift through the night.

Turn to page 3.

In the morning, the storm has died out. But you do not have much strength left. In the dawn light, you no longer see any sign of the ship. You wonder how far you have drifted.

You hope there are no sharks in this part of the ocean. Sadly you realize that without fresh water, you cannot live much longer anyway.

You drift for hours until, late in the afternoon, you spot something on the horizon. Land! You abandon your barrel and start to swim. Before long, you see a mountain island rising up out of the mist.

With the last bit of your strength used up, you let the gentle waves wash you up on the bright, sandy beach.

After you have rested, you begin to walk unsteadily down the beach. You climb up on a big rock. Far down the shore stands a man!

The man, who looks like a native, is hunting for crabs. He carries a spear. You wonder if he is friendly or hostile.

If you want to go to this man, turn to page 6.

If you want to avoid this man, and go into the island forest, turn to page 9.

from page 64

You follow the man into the jungle. He does not turn to talk to you, but walks calmly along the jungle path.

Turn to page 87.

You run to the nearest tree. The boar chases you, but you scramble up the tree just in time. Soon the boar loses interest in you, and walks away into the jungle. Now that you are safe, you climb a bit higher in the tree. Perhaps you can get a good view of the entire island.

Suddenly you hear voices below. You look down to see a gang of men, carrying a big wooden chest and shovels. They walk through the glade below, not noticing you above.

If you want to follow these men, turn to page 44.

If you want to stay hidden in the tree, turn to page 53.

from page 3

Delighted to see another human being, you walk down the beach toward the crab-hunter. But as you approach, he sees you, picks up his catch, and walks away into the jungle. You call after him, but soon he disappears among the trees.

If you want to follow him, turn to page 12.

If you want to keep walking along the beach, turn to page 18.

A sound wakes you in the middle of the night. But you don't know what kind of sound it was—the roar of an animal, the cry of a bird, or a human voice? You turn to ask Zeke, but he is gone!

If you want to go out into the forest, turn to page 56.

If you want to stay in the hut, turn to page 91.

from page 3

Although you are happy to see another human being, you do not want to take a chance yet on meeting him. You walk into the forest, through beautiful groves of ebony, mango, and palm trees. You pick fruit as you see it: bananas, plantains, and coconuts. It all tastes delicious.

You were soaking wet when you arrived on the island. But soon the warm sun dries you. You are happy to be alive. You have not slept all night, so you find a safe spot overlooking the ocean and fall asleep.

A noise wakes you. It takes just a moment to remember where you are. You do not know how long you have been asleep. Now you see what woke you. A wild boar has wandered by and is rooting around for food.

If you want to run for the nearest tree, turn to page 5.

If you want to remain silent and still, turn to page 70.

10

You tell Odette about how you were shipwrecked, and about how you came to this island and found her tree house.

She is interested in your entire story. Then she tells you hers: "Until several years ago, I lived in a large city and worked for an insurance company. When I received a small inheritance, I quit my job, left the city, and came to this island, the first one I saw after leaving California.

"Now a ship stops here every six months and drops off the painting supplies I need."

Turn to page 29.

The ape looks at you not with anger but with curiosity. You are very scared, until you notice that the ape is unhappy. You soon see why. It has a thorn in its hand that it cannot remove. The miserable ape suddenly puts you back on the ground. On the ground, you see some human footprints.

If you want to follow the footprints into the jungle, turn to page 41.

If you want to try to help the ape, turn to page 89.

from page 6

You enter the edge of the jungle, but the man is nowhere to be seen. You walk through the cool shade, happy to be out of the sunlight. As you walk, you begin to remember how hungry you are.

Then, as if you had asked for food out loud, you spot a bunch of ripe bananas lying in the middle of the path.

If you want to eat the bananas, turn to page 20.

If you do not want to eat the bananas, turn to page 39.

You stay with Lila and the villagers. You learn to hunt the wild boar, how to fish, how to catch crabs.

After a few days pass, you begin to feel stronger. The fresh air and sunshine helps you feel much better.

Lila begins to teach you her language. And soon you are talking with the other islanders, learning from them. You teach the children games from your country.

Months go by. One day you are searching for crabs on the beach. It is a beautiful, sunny day. Then you see it: a sailing ship anchoring offshore.

If you want to signal to the ship, turn to page 55.

If you want to hide and remain on the island, turn to page 57.

14

You decide to swim the short distance out to the atoll. The water is warm and crystal-clear. You can see a school of bluefish. Perhaps tonight you can catch a crab, or some other tasty sea creature.

When you reach the small island, you are careful not to cut your feet on the sharp coral. You climb to the center of the island and rest on a grassy hill beneath some palm trees. From here you have a good view of the main island.

Finding several ripe coconuts, you eat one hungrily and hide the rest. When night falls, you are exhausted. You fall sound asleep.

In the morning, a voice wakes you. "Ahoy!"

You wake to meet two men standing before you. One looks like a native of the South Seas. He is tall and is dressed like an American sailor. The other man is also tall, with long hair and a dark beard. He wears a coat of blue with brass buttons. One of his legs is made of wood. Both men are slightly wet and sunburned.

Turn to page 22.

16

You follow the path in the direction of the noise. Soon you hear it again. This time you recognize the sound of a man moaning softly. You walk ahead and see a man lying in the path. It is Zeke, and he is hurt. You rush over to him.

"Get help," says Zeke. "Follow this path. Get help from the chief—Orin." He is too weak to tell you anything else.

If you want to follow the path to find Orin, turn to page 99.

If you want to go look for whoever did this, turn to page 35.

You decide to remain in the jungle. You have come to feel this is your home. You love to swing through the trees and feel the warm sun on your head. Off you swing with the great ape, singing out a joyful song to the forest.

THE END

18

As you walk down the beach, you begin to think. If there are other people on the island, will they also be unfriendly? Could you be in danger? Perhaps you should find a place to hide while you try to think of a way to be rescued.

Looking out at the ocean, you now see an atoll, a narrow coral island. Coconut trees grow there. You will have to swim a short way to get to the atoll, but you will probably be safe there.

Now you see something else. On the sand in front of you are human footprints. Somehow you know they do not belong to the islander you just saw. The prints lead into the jungle.

If you want to swim for the atoll, turn to page 14.

If you want to follow the footprints, turn to page 41.

Playing and living with Mako has been fun, but your Uncle Jack is probably very worried about you. You ask Mako to take you down to the ship, then tell him to stay out of sight. You do not want him to be hunted or captured by the sailors. He will always be your secret friend, and you promise that you will come back soon to visit him.

Then you signal to the ship. The captain of the ship rescues you and takes you to Pago Pago. From there you find a ship to take you to Australia. It is a pleasant voyage, but the sailors worry a bit about the way you joyfully swing from mast to mast.

You have had a wonderful adventure.

THE END

20

As you pick up the bananas, a rope grabs you around the ankles, then lifts you upside-down in the air. All at once, five hunters appear. They seem surprised to see you in the trap. They take you down, but instead of setting you free, they tie you upside-down to a pole and carry you along the jungle path.

The men bring you to their camp. There are many thatched huts, with many small children running about. You would normally be interested in learning about this new culture. But right now all you can think about is whether you will be cooked for dinner. The hunters seem to be discussing just what to do with you.

Turn to page 34.

from page 14

"Ahoy, there," says the man with the wooden leg. "Perhaps we were all wrecked in the same storm two days back. My name is Peter, and this is my friend, Teego."

You ask them to sit down with you.

"We drifted here in our lifeboat," says Peter. "Are there any other people on this island?"

You tell them all you know, about the man with the spear, and how you swam here for safety.

Teego and Peter are interested to hear this. But something else is on Peter's mind. Finally he says, "Have you got anything to eat?"

Turn to page 86.

Three islanders appear out of the bushes. They carry no weapons, and they want you to go with them.

If you want to go with these men, turn to page 66.

If you want to run away into the jungle, turn to page 76.

Something draws you to the beach. When you get there, you see an empty rowboat dragged up on the sand. Offshore, a naval ship is anchored.

If you would like to take the rowboat out to the ship, turn to page 42.

If you would like to wait for the owner of the boat to return, turn to page 63.

You want to be rescued more than anything else, so you tell Lila that you must leave tomorrow morning.

When you wake up the next morning, the villagers feed you a delicious, hot breakfast. They are sad to see you go. Lila guides you to the edge of their territory. Then you thank her and say good-bye.

Turn to page 28.

from page 37

You run and hide with Peter and Teego in the woods. "I just hope they didn't see us," says Peter. A long rowboat leaves the ship and rows to the beach near you. Five men get out. Two of them carry a huge chest.

Peter says, "That's Graybeard, the leader. The most evil man to sail the seven seas. He's come to bury his treasure on this island.

"Those poor devils with him must be his prisoners. I know his tricks. Graybeard will take them to a lonely place on the island and tell them to dig a deep hole. After they finish digging, he'll kill them all and bury them with the treasure."

"We've got to stop them," you say.

"How can we? The man is ruthless. And we have no weapons."

All at once, the three of you are surrounded. Not by pirates, but by islanders, pointing sharp spears at you.

"Rats," says Peter.

But Teego speaks to one of the natives in a language you have never heard before. The islander answers Teego, and they begin to talk.

Turn to page 50.

28

As you walk through the jungle, you nibble on fruit and berries whenever you feel hungry. The island has lost some of its strangeness. The sun warms you. You walk comfortably until the sun begins to set.

You must find a safe place to spend the night. As you watch the beautiful sunset, you see small, blinking lights moving at high speed over the island.

Suddenly one of the lights falls behind the others. It begins to soar toward you. You take cover as the blue light crashes in the jungle behind you. It makes hardly a sound as it swishes through the trees and lands with a dull thud.

You hurry through the bushes, led by the throbbing blue light.

Turn to page 96.

from page 10

"This island is not far from the captain's course to Australia. His ship is due here in a few days. Why don't you stay with me until then? I would very much like to paint your portrait."

You agree to stay and have your portrait painted. Soon you will be rescued.

You ask Odette to tell you about the island.

"There are more people here than just the man you saw on the beach. The islanders are the best people, the kindest I've ever met. I've learned to speak their language. They did not understand at first why I had come here. But now they accept me. And as you can see, they let me paint them.

"You should meet them before you leave. I can teach you some phrases." Odette teaches you as she paints. "Remember, if you ever need help, just whistle." She whistles. "Only ten times louder!"

Several delightful days pass, and finally the painting is done. It is an excellent likeness of you, full of lush color. The background of palm trees and ferns makes you look a bit like a native islander yourself.

Turn to page 30.

30

"Sleep well, my friend," says Odette. "Tomorrow, the ship should arrive. If all the people back home were as delightful as you, perhaps I never would have left."

In the middle of the night, something wakes you. You notice that Odette is gone. You are alone in the tree house.

There are two men speaking quietly below, unaware of the tree house above them. They are each holding a lit torch.

"I tell you, this is the path to the site."

"No, it isn't. The path is closer to the beach."

"We should never have come at night. What are we going to do with that woman?"

"Let me handle that."

They walk away.

Is Odette in trouble? You decide to climb down the tree and follow the men.

Turn to page 32.

32

You climb down, hoping you can help Odette before it is too late. For you are sure it was she they were talking about.

It is easy to follow the men with the torches. They are looking for something. Finally they seem to find it.

"This is it," says one. "I would remember this place even in the dark. Let's dig it up, then get rid of the woman and leave."

Unfortunately, you creep too close. One of the men spots you in the torchlight. "Hey!" he shouts.

You run back into the forest, back along the path. The men are running after you. Maybe you can make it back to the tree house.

If you want to whistle as you run, turn to page 51.

If you want to run off the path and hide in the bushes, turn to page 90.

from page 44

You are afraid for your own life, so you do nothing. The captain shoots his own men, then buries them with the treasure. Now there is nothing you can do but watch as he returns to his ship. You are left on the island, alone.

THE END

from page 20

In the end, the men untie you and put you inside one of their huts. They give you fruit that tastes very good.

Soon night falls, yet no one seems to be guarding you. At last a woman enters your hut and speaks in your language. "My name is Lila," she says. "Long ago, when I was a girl, a woman came over the water and lived with us. She taught me how to speak her language. Now you have come. Will you also stay with us? I can teach you our language. You can be happy here."

"Thank you, Lila," you say. "But I think my own family will miss me. Do any other people live on this island? Do boats ever come here?"

Lila tells you that sometimes boats do come, usually to the other side of the island. "But please do not go there. There is danger. Please stay with us—do not go!"

If you want to stay with Lila for a while, turn to page 13.

If you want to go to the other side of the island, turn to page 25.

from page 16

You are so angry at whoever did this to Zeke that you run in the direction of a nearby torchlight. But when you get too close, you realize your foolhardiness. Four men see you at once. The last thing you remember is the bright night of shining stars.

THE END

from page 47

You are so hungry that you cannot wait any longer. You climb down the ladder and soon find all the coconuts you can eat. After eating the delicious fruit, you wonder what you should do next. How long will it take the artist to return?

If you want to go back up to the tree house to wait, turn to page 79.

If you want to explore more of the jungle, turn to page 28.

You decide to go in the small rowboat with Peter and Teego. The three of you row to the mainland, and hide the boat in a small cove. Soon you find more coconuts, and bananas. You sit on the beach, start a fire with Teego's help, cook some crabs and eat a delicious meal, the first good meal you have had in days.

You are glad you came with the two ex-pirates. They argue and joke about science and philosophy. They trade terrible puns. You enjoy being in their company.

As you are laughing at one of Teego's stories, you find yourself laughing alone. You look at the two of them, and they are staring out to sea. You turn around and see it—a ship!

But Peter and Teego are scared. "That's Graybeard's ship. Hide!" They run as fast as they can up the beach into the forest. They did not stay long enough to say who Graybeard is.

If you want to run and hide with Peter and Teego, turn to page 27.

If you want to signal to the ship, turn to page 58.

from page 12

You do not feel right about taking these bananas. You are suspicious. It just looks as if someone put the bananas there. If you are going to survive on this island, you cannot fall into a hunter's trap.

You leave the path and slip into the forest.

"It was wise of you not to take those bananas," says a voice from behind a bush. You look to see a bearded man wearing an old straw hat.

"I see that you're shipwrecked," says the man. "Well, don't worry, there's plenty of other food here. Come on." He turns and walks through the jungle.

If you want to follow the man, turn to page 87.

If you want to stay on your own, turn to page 28.

40

from page 82

You go off in search of water. Soon you hear a familiar sound: the surf. You have found the ocean. Clutching the map, you walk out of the forest.

There you see sailors on the beach! One of them is a naval captain. He and his crew have rowed ashore in their longboat to bring back fresh water to their ship. They have found a stream not far from where you are. This is your chance to be rescued. But what are you going to do about the treasure map?

If you want to be rescued, but want to keep the secret to yourself, turn to page 46.

If you want to be rescued and let the sailors in on the secret, turn to page 93.

If you do not want to reveal yourself, but want to go back to find the treasure after the men leave, turn to page 101.

from page 11 / from page 18

You follow the footprints, and they lead to a pleasant path. Tall trees block the hot sunlight. You have not walked far when you find a surprise: a rope ladder hanging from a tree. Up in the tree rests a tree house.

Turn to page 47.

42

from page 24 / from page 63

You decide to take the rowboat out to the ship. Perhaps the noise you heard was the person who came over from the big ship. You row out, and the watchman spots you. Several sailors help you aboard.

You explain that you are shipwrecked, that you only borrowed this rowboat to be rescued.

The officer in charge tells you that four deserters took the boat only an hour ago. No one knows why they left, but the sailors are glad to see the deserters gone.

You hope Zeke will be all right. The next morning, you set sail for Tahiti, where you will be able to catch a new ship for Australia.

THE END

"In fact, until a couple of days ago we were robbing ships all over the Pacific," says Peter. "But we never hurt anyone, I swear it.

"Then the storm came. It wrecked our ship and took the lives of everyone on board but our own. Call it fate, but I believe Teego and I were rescued for some reason. I don't believe I can ever go back to my old ways.

"Now that you know this, there is no reason for you to trust us. Most people don't change their ways so easily. I just think that since we're all in this together, we ought to join forces. There's lots of things we can do to get rescued. The first thing we should do is make a signal. And we should do that from the main island, not from this little atoll. There's probably more food on the island, too. What do you say? Will you come with us?"

If you want to go back with Peter and Teego to the main island, turn to page 37.

If you want to remain by yourself on the atoll, turn to page 98.

44

Hoping for a chance to be rescued, you follow these men. But you are cautious. You have read enough books to know something about pirates, and these men look suspicious to you.

They are making a lot of noise, so you are able to follow them in secret. When they get to a small clearing, they put down the chest and start digging a hole. They dig deeper and deeper. You stay hidden.

When the hole is finished, the leader says to the diggers in the hole: "Thank you, mates. Now I am afraid I must shoot you. We can't have too many people know where this treasure is buried. And I only trust myself. So good-bye."

If you want to try to stop the leader, turn to page 100.

If you want to do nothing, turn to page 33.

from page 40

You confront the captain and tell him about how you were shipwrecked. But you do not tell him about the treasure map. Perhaps someday you can come back to this island. For now, you are just happy to be on your way home.

THE END

47

from page 41

You climb the ladder and peek into the small house. There is no one home. There are a few pieces of primitive but comfortable furniture. But the house is mostly filled with tubes of paint, brushes, old cans, and paintings.

Some of the paintings are of tropical fruit or jungle scenes or the beach. But most are portraits of native people, like the man you saw. There are pictures of different men, women, and children. The deep, rich colors make them look so peaceful and beautiful. Now you are just a bit sorry you did not get to talk to the man on the beach.

What you are most curious about is who did these paintings. You hope the owner of the house will return soon. Happily, the paint on the palette is still wet. The painter has not been gone long. As you wait, you remember how hungry you are. You have not eaten anything since yesterday.

If you want to climb down the ladder to find some food, turn to page 36.

If you want to wait in the tree house for the owner to return, turn to page 79.

from page 81

You run after Teego. But as you run, you see you will not be able to help the tall islander. Graybeard is almost at the beach.

Then something lucky happens. The captain runs into an animal snare. He trips the trigger. A rope grabs his ankle and lifts him upside-down, high up in a tree.

You and Teego pick up the captain's gun.

"Don't call for help, or you'll be sorry," you tell Graybeard.

Now that you have the pirate leader, it will be easy to make the other pirates on the ship cooperate with you. They are cowards without their boss.

Each of you gets an equal share of the pirates' treasure. You thank the islanders for their help, then prepare to leave on the former pirate ship. Peter and Teego take command.

"Ahoy!" calls Peter. "Off to Australia!"

THE END

from page 27

After a short conversation, Teego says to you and Peter, "I have told these good people how we came here, and I have also told them about Graybeard.

"They already know about Graybeard," says Teego. "Others of their people are following him now. They will help us if they can, but they will not harm anyone, and they will not allow *us* to harm anyone. It is against the law of their gods."

"Not much help, are they?" grumbles Peter.

"But there are now many of us," you say. "That's the important thing." You tell them a plan you have, and you go off to try to rescue the prisoners.

Turn to page 68.

from page 32

As you run, you give a loud whistle. But nothing happens. You keep running, and the men are gaining on you. You don't know where you are.

Suddenly you are tangled in thick vines. The men are almost upon you. Then two hands grab you from above, and lift you up into a tree. Two islanders are holding you, looking at you with their calm, clear eyes. They motion to you to climb farther up the tree with them.

Turn to page 69.

You climb to the topmost branches of the tree. From this perch, you can see in every direction. The island is much bigger than you thought, with its tall mountains in the middle. Next, you look out at the ocean. There is a sailing ship, which must have brought the men you just saw.

This ship gives you much to think about. The ship is not flying the flag of any nation. Could it be a pirate ship? Those men with the wooden chest certainly could have been pirates.

You decide to climb carefully down the tree and walk to the beach for a closer look. What if the people on the ship *are* pirates? They would have to have the decency to rescue you from this island, wouldn't they?

When you get to the beach, you suddenly feel a hand on your shoulder.

Turn to page 64.

54

from page 74 / from page 80

You wander into the forest on your own and begin to feel more at ease. You make a small hut for yourself in the jungle, build a fire, catch small animals, and gather fruits. You never see another ship come to the island. But you make this place your home.

THE END

from page 13

You signal to the ship, and they send a rowboat to pick you up. The sailors are pleased to rescue you. They want to hear your story.

Much has happened in the months that you were gone. You are a little sad to leave your island paradise. But you hope you can bring back to a troubled world what you have learned about living a life of peace.

THE END

56

from page 7

What if it was Zeke's voice you heard? You must go out and look, despite his warning. The stars overhead are brighter than you have ever seen them. The moon helps you find your way down the old path.

Where could Zeke be? Now the path comes to a fork. One way leads to where you thought you heard the noise. The other way leads down to the beach. From where you stand, you can see the nearby ocean. You can see a ship just offshore, with its lights burning.

If you want to go toward the noise, turn to page 16.

If you want to go to the beach, turn to page 24.

from page 13

___

You hide in the forest, so the sailors on the boat do not spot you. Maybe someday you will be ready to go back to civilization. But for now, your home is with the peaceful villagers on your island paradise.

THE END

58

from page 37

You signal to the ship. Peter and Teego are out of sight. Already the ship has spotted you, and is sending out a rowboat with several men aboard.

You stand on the beach, delighted that you are going to be rescued so soon. Unfortunately the men are pirates, and they are looking for a new person to work in their kitchen. The last person did not wash the dishes well enough, and he was fed to the sharks. Now they take you back to their ship, to see if you will do a better job. They give you a lifetime position.

THE END

from page 64

As the man disappears into the trees, you signal to the ship. The men on board send a rowboat to get you. Yes, they are pirates, and yes, they will take you with them.

They are more than glad to have you: to work in the galley, to wash their dishes, and to scrub the deck. You may be a member of this unhappy crew for a long time to come.

THE END

from page 70

You follow the footprints through the jungle. You are on your guard, listening for the slightest noise. The jungle is hot, and your progress is slow. Whatever you are following can take great strides through the thick-growing plants. Finally you sit down to take a rest.

But no sooner have you stopped than a giant hand picks you up into the air. The hand belongs to a giant ape, which stands over thirty feet tall. It bares its teeth at you.

Turn to page 11.

from page 96

You run and hide in the jungle, and you do not stop running until you are far from the crash site. When you return half an hour later, you find no sign of the blue people or their ship.

Now it is getting dark, and you are alone in the jungle.

Or are you alone? You think you can see many pairs of eyes looking at you from behind the jungle leaves.

THE END

You do not think it would be right to take this boat. It must belong to someone. You wait about half an hour, but no one appears. You wonder about the noise you heard. Could that noise have been made by the person who owns the boat?

If you want to go down the path where you might have heard the noise, turn to page 16.

If you want to change your mind and take the rowboat out to the ship, turn to page 42.

from page 53

You turn around and face a tall man with a long beard. He is wearing a cap made of leaves, and a pair of carefully mended, sun-bleached pants.

"They are bad men," he says slowly, looking at the ship. "Come walk with me." He turns around and walks lightly toward the forest.

If you want to go with the man, turn to page 4.

If you want to signal to the ship, turn to page 59.

from page 74

You agree to help the men, and you come up with a plan. Everyone agrees to your idea. You tie up the captain, then wait till dark.

You and the four sailors get into the rowboat and row out to the ship. You take the drunken pirate crew by surprise. Some of the pirates join you. The others you lock in the hold. Then you go back to retrieve the treasure and the captain.

The next day you set sail for Samoa, where you will be able to book first-class passage on to Australia. You are wiser and richer than when you started out. You arrive at your aunt and uncle's house only a few weeks late, and they are delighted to see you.

THE END

66

from page 23

You let these men escort you along a hidden jungle path. Because they speak a different language, you cannot ask them anything.

Soon you are led into a great village of thatched huts. The men lead you through a great gate. The village is a kind of fortress, guarded by a tall wall of upright tree trunks. You wonder if the wall is to keep out whatever made the huge footprints outside.

You are brought before the village leader. To your astonishment, she speaks your language.

"Welcome to our village," she says. "The hunters say you were lost in the jungle. We would like to offer you our help. You may stay with us here, if you like."

Then a young woman walks up to the leader. The young woman is crying. She speaks in a hurried plea. The chief listens, then translates for you. "The Great Ape has taken her two children. None of our hunters will try to save them on the night of a full moon. That is taboo. But tomorrow it may be too late to save them."

If you want to offer to rescue the two children, turn to page 85.

If you want to do nothing right now, turn to page 77.

from page 50

When you sneak up on Graybeard, the prisoners are almost finished digging their pit. Now Teego gives a bird call. Graybeard looks up. You give an animal cry, then shout from behind a tree, "Graybeard!"

The islanders all begin to make noises, according to your plan. Graybeard sees he is outnumbered. He shoots wildly and runs away into the jungle. The natives allow him to pass through their ring unharmed. He runs toward the beach.

Turn to page 81.

from page 51

You climb the tree with the two islanders, higher and higher. The men below fire guns at you. One bullet whistles by your ear. But suddenly the shooting stops. In a moment, the islanders help you back down the tree. You look around, but the strangers are gone. The two islanders do not seem to be troubled. Did other islanders take care of the strangers? You may never know.

The two islanders bring you back to the tree house, and there you find Odette. She had been out for a moonlight stroll when she met the two strangers. They were looking for stolen treasure. Before she had a chance to whistle for help, she was captured by the men.

You all go back to the village for a midnight feast. You spend the next day with the villagers, looking after Odette and keeping her company. Soon she feels better.

At last, the supply ship arrives, and you bid a fond farewell to your artist friend. You promise to come back to visit. Odette gives you a present—the beautiful portrait she painted of you. You are on your way to Australia!

THE END

70

You do not dare to move, for fear of alarming the boar. Luckily the animal seems more interested in looking for other kinds of food. It sniffs around and around.

Then you hear something else: a dull thud, repeated every two seconds. The earth shakes. The boar hears the noise, then runs quickly into the underbrush. You are left alone. Then the noise stops.

You creep through the dense trees and bushes. Suddenly you see freshly broken branches. In front of you is a large footprint, bigger than any footprint you have ever seen. Fifteen yards ahead is another print.

If you want to follow these footprints, turn to page 61.

If you want to get away from the prints, turn to page 23.

from page 89

When you wake up the next morning, you are in the heart of the jungle. You see giant reptiles roaming about. Most seem peaceful. You learn how to swing from tree to tree using long vines. You climb mountains and swim across rivers. You get stronger and healthier every day. A week goes by, and soon you are even able to communicate with the ape, whom you call Mako.

One day, about a month later, you and Mako are near the highest peak of the island mountain chain. You spot a ship offshore.

If you want Mako to take you down to the ship, turn to page 19.

If you want to remain in the jungle with Mako, turn to page 17.

from page 99

When you wake up, it is day. Zeke and Orin, and a man in a naval officer's uniform stand over you. You are in a primitive hut.

"You've done well," says Zeke. "Orin and her people stopped the men who hurt me last night. Now I feel much better."

"Who were the men?" you ask.

"They were deserters from my ship," says the officer. "Their heads were filled with crazy ideas about buried treasure on this island."

"Of course, there is no treasure on this island," says Zeke. He thanks you for helping him and congratulates you now that you can be rescued.

You are sorry to say good-bye to Orin and Zeke. On your way down to the beach, to the waiting ship, Zeke slips you a gold coin. He winks, as if to say, "Let this be our secret." You promise to come back and visit someday.

THE END

74

from page 100

You confront the thankful men.

"We are not pirates," they say. "We are captured sailors. Listen—there is plenty of treasure in this chest, and you are entitled to an equal share of it. But we must act fast. We can take the pirates' ship and see to it that the captain is brought back to trial. Will you help us one more time?"

If you want to help these men, turn to page 65.

If you do not want to join them, turn to page 54.

from page 82

You decide to follow the map and try to find the treasure first. With any luck, you will find a stream on the way. Although you do not find water, you soon find the place on the map where the treasure is supposed to be buried.

You dig and you dig. The heat of the jungle gets worse. Too late, you realize that you have lost too much fluid. You leave the site in search of a stream, clutching the map in your hands. But you never make it. Twentieth-century explorers find your bones.

THE END

from page 23

You run as quickly as you can, deeper and deeper into the jungle. You pause to listen for any noise following you, but the jungle is silent. Tall trees loom overhead. You are tired, but you do not want to fall asleep in the jungle. You walk and walk, and do not know if you have the strength to go much farther.

Turn to page 82.

from page 66

You do not think you can do anything to help the children. You start to live with the villagers from that day onward. The children are never found, but you soon become an accepted member of the tribe. You learn to hunt, to fish, and to survive. It is a difficult but peaceful life.

THE END

You decide to wait in the tree house for the artist to return. An hour passes, but still no artist.

You look at the brushes and tubes of paint. The labels say they were made in the United States. How did they get here?

There are so many painting supplies, you begin to wonder if you'd like to start doing a painting of your own, to help pass the time. Finally you give in. You begin to paint a picture of the artist's studio, with its colorful paint tubes, canvases, frames, and palm-leaf walls. You get absorbed in your creation. Finally it is finished.

"That is beautiful," says a voice behind you. You turn in surprise to see a woman admiring your painting. You try to apologize.

"Oh, no. I'm delighted. It isn't often that I get visitors from the outside world. Welcome to my home. My name is Odette. Please tell me all about yourself, but first let's have tea . . . ."

Turn to page 10.

80

You run back into the forest, wanting nothing more to do with pirates. They do not follow you.

Turn to page 54.

You have saved the prisoners! But Graybeard is now getting away. You will all be left stranded on the island, no better off than before. Worse yet, the captain will be back with his pirates. After all, you have his treasure.

Peter, the sailors, and the villagers want to hide. But suddenly Teego runs after Graybeard.

"Come back, Teego!" cries Peter. "What's come over you?"

If you want to hide with everyone else, turn to page 94.

If you want to run after Teego, turn to page 48.

Soon you come upon an amazing discovery—the skeleton of a man holding a sword. You wonder how long ago this man came here, and who he was. A rusted shovel lies nearby. In the other hand he clutches a bottle.

Inside the sealed bottle is a map, a treasure map, which claims to lead to a treasure on the side of the mountain. You could find it without much trouble, using landmarks. This man probably just did not make it, for bad luck or some other reason. You hope your strength holds out. Right now you would pay a fortune just for a cool glass of water.

If you want to try to find water first, turn to page 40.

If you want to look for the treasure first, turn to page 75.

84

You grab the three small people. They are still in shock. You hide behind some coral rock formations. The loud noise is getting closer. Then an animal appears—a gigantic lizard that walks on its two hind legs. The lizard picks up the metal ship, but then drops it like a hot potato and goes bounding off into the forest.

Turn to page 95.

from page 66

This person needs help, and you want to do whatever you can.

Although you don't know where to look for the great ape, the chief gives you a guide who will show you the way. Tash is his name.

Tash leads you deeper and deeper into the jungle. Suddenly he points ahead. You see the ape—a giant gorilla at least thirty feet tall, carrying the two small children in its huge hand. You can never hope to rescue the children now. Then you get some luck: the animal puts the children down. You don't know why the ape has taken the children, but you see your chance to rescue them.

You creep up while the ape is looking away. You grab the children, but the ape sees you. It picks you up high in the air. The children run to Tash, and together they disappear into the jungle.

Turn to page 11.

86

from page 22

You are not sure if you can trust Peter and Teego, but you do want to help them. You give them your hidden food and they eat hungrily.

"Thank you," says Teego.

"Listen," says Peter. "You've helped us and I'm grateful. I think we owe it to you to be honest. You see, Teego and I are *pirates*."

Turn to page 43.

The man leads you to a small, thatched hut in the forest.

"Come eat lunch with me," he says. "Then tell me your story."

You eagerly accept his invitation. Then you tell him the story of how you were shipwrecked.

"Something like that happened to me years ago," says the man. "That's how I came to this island. Oh, I've had chances to be rescued since then. The outside world visits this island more and more these days. But I don't want to go back. This is my home now."

You introduce yourself.

"Call me Zeke," says the man. "That's my name, though I haven't used it for years."

You are glad to hear that he has had chances to be rescued. You ask him for more information.

"Ships stop here for water," says Zeke. "Or to bury things," he adds with a knowing look. "But you're safe now. Feel free to stay with me as long as you like. There are many good people that live on this island, only a few not-so-good."

You talk all afternoon. When the sun at last begins to set, Zeke gets ready to go to sleep. He puts some extra wood on the fire, then says good night. "You can stay awake as long as you like," he says. "Whatever you do, just don't go out into the jungle at night."

Turn to page 7.

from page 11

You try to pull the thorn out of the ape's hand. The ape howls, but sees you are trying to help. Finally you succeed. The ape picks you up again! It carries you through the jungle, holding you gently in its giant hand. How wonderful it is to look out over the trees.

Deeper and deeper into the heart of the jungle you go. There are no paths here. The trees are getting taller. You see giant reptiles, some bigger than elephants. The trees are so big that the ape can now swing from branch to branch. He covers great distances in a single leap.

Finally, in one tall tree, you arrive in the ape's home. The ape offers you as many bananas as you can eat. You are so tired, you soon fall sound asleep.

Turn to page 71.

from page 32

Desperate to lose the men, you leap into the bushes. Unfortunately, they see you and leap after you.

You whistle for help, but it is too late. The islanders will always tell legends about you, the friend of Odette the painter.

THE END

from page 7

You remember Zeke's warning about not leaving the tent at night. The fire outside your hut burns brightly, but you are all alone. You try to go back to sleep.

The next morning, Zeke does not return. You keep yourself busy looking for food and tending the fire, but your new friend never comes back.

Eventually you make the hut your own home. As the months and years go by, you also forget about civilization. You feel more and more comfortable in your island paradise, but you will always be haunted by the strange night when Zeke disappeared.

THE END

from page 40

You confront the sailors and tell them how you were shipwrecked. You also tell them about the treasure map you found. You offer to share half of whatever treasure you find.

The captain agrees to spend the extra day on the island to make the search. As you lead them to the site, you find the three coral stones marked on the map. You all begin to dig on the side of the mountain.

Near the surface you find several gold coins. You dig steadily. Finally you hit a wooden wall. You break down the wall and find a room. Inside is a wooden chest, containing much gold and jewels. Half of this enormous fortune is yours.

The sailors drop you and your treasure off in Tahiti. From here you can catch a new ship on to Australia. You are rich!

THE END

from page 81

You, Peter, and the sailors go hide with the villagers deep in the forest. The pirates will never find you here. From the beach, you hear the sounds of gunfire, then all is quiet. Night comes, and so does Teego. He tried but failed to stop Graybeard from getting away. When you return to the treasure site the next day, the treasure is gone. So is the pirate ship.

You are glad to have the company of Peter and Teego, and to meet the friendly islanders. But you hope that someday another ship will come. For now, all you can do is wait.

THE END

When the blue people feel better, they speak to you in your own language. "Thank you, earthling, for your act of kindness."

Soon red lights appear over the ocean. A red ship is coming to the rescue. The blue people say good-bye as they beam up to the red ship. You only wish that someone could rescue *you*.

Then, almost as if someone had read your thoughts, *you* are beamed up into the red ship. You do not remember much after that. But almost immediately you find yourself on your aunt and uncle's farm in Australia—one week before your expected arrival.

Because you don't think your aunt and uncle will believe how you got there so quickly, you tell them you took an early ship. Uncle Jack and Aunt Kate really don't care—they are just delighted to have you. You are glad all your strange adventures are over. But every night, after everyone else has gone to sleep, you look out of your second-floor window, hoping to see colored lights in the Australian sky.

THE END

96

from page 28

When you get as close as you can to the blue light, you see it is a metal ship. Small, blue people are coming out of the ship's doorway, holding their heads in their hands. Each blue person is about three feet tall, with large eyes and ears. There are three of these people in all. As you look on in wonder, you hear the sound of a big animal coming your way.

If you want to run and hide, turn to page 62.

If you want to try to hide the aliens, turn to page 84.

from page 43

You decide to remain on the atoll, alone. You just don't believe that Peter and Teego will change their ways that quickly.

So you remain on the atoll, as Peter and Teego row off in their boat. They seem genuinely sad that you won't come with them. That is the last you ever see of them. The next day, when there is no more food to be found on the atoll, you too swim back to the main island. You live there for many years, on your own tropical island.

THE END

You rush down the path. But you have no idea what you are supposed to say to Chief Orin. How can you ask for help if you do not speak the same language? You soon find the village, and ask a young woman if she knows Orin.

"I am Orin," she says in perfect English.

You try to hide your surprise. "Zeke sent me," you say. "He is hurt."

Orin whistles. Soon many other islanders—men and women—gather at her side. Together, you run down the path towards Zeke. Unfortunately you do not see as well in the dark as the islanders do. As they turn a sharp corner, you trip over a rock. That is the last thing you remember.

Turn to page 73.

from page 44

You can't stand to see this murder occur, so you cry out, "Stop! Don't shoot!" The captain wheels around, surprised at hearing another voice. He now aims his gun at you. But that gives the men in the hole time to throw a rock at him and knock him out. The men tie up the captain.

If you want to confront these men, turn to page 74.

If you want to run back into the forest, turn to page 80.

from page 40

You do not want to talk to these men, because they will surely want part or all of your treasure. You hide until the men leave. You drink the water you need, then go back into the jungle. You find the treasure, and it is a magnificent one. But you are never able to get off of the island to use it.

THE END